# Field Trip

# More Super♡Duper♡Royal♡Deluxe books!

# Missy's
## Super ♡ Duper ♡ Royal ♡ Deluxe

# Field Trip
### By
### Susan Nees

BRANCHES
SCHOLASTIC INC.

# For Samuel and Benjamin

Photocredits:
pp. 18-19: © bomberclaad/istockphoto

Library of Congress Cataloging-in-Publication Data

Nees, Susan, author.
Field trip / by Susan Nees.
pages cm. — (Missy's super duper royal deluxe ; 4) (Branches)
Summary: On a school field trip to the state Capitol, Missy is
dissapointed to learn that there is no gift shop and decides,
along with her friend Oscar, to visit the governor to petition one.
ISBN 0-545-43854-3 (pbk. : alk. paper) — ISBN 0-545-49612-8 (hardcover: alk paper) — ISBN 0-545-57704-7 (ebook) 1. School field trips—Juvenile fiction. 2. Gift shops—Juvenile fiction. [1. School field trips—Fiction. 2. Gift shops—Fiction.] I. Title. II. Series: Nees, Susan. Missy's super duper royal deluxe ; 4. III. Series: Branches (Scholastic Inc.)
PZ7.N384Fi 2014
[E]—dc23

                        2013027607

ISBN 978-0-545-49612-4 (hardcover) / ISBN 978-0-545-43854-4 (paperback)

12 11 10 9 8 7                              16 17 18 19/0

Printed in China                   38
First Scholastic printing, December 2013

Book design by Marissa Asuncion

# Table of Contents

# Chapter One
## Happy Dance

This is Melissa Abigail Rose.

But everyone calls her "Missy."

This is Missy's cat Pink.

Everyone calls him "Pink."

When Missy woke up this morning, she did her happy dance.

Hip hip hooray!

I can't wait!

Today is the field trip!

It is going to be super duper fun!

Missy's class was going on a field trip to the state capitol. A field trip meant a bus ride and special snacks and no schoolwork.

And most exciting of all, a field trip meant a gift shop!

snow globe

stickers

glitter pens

charm bracelet

glasses

pinwheel

super duper
hat

Once Missy got to school, she lined up by the bus. The class had to wait for their teacher, Miss Snodgrass, to call out partners for the day.

Quiet down. Let's get started.

Miss Snodgrass called out the partners, two by two.

Paulette and Dexter.

Tiffany and Taylor.

Josey and Lily.

Missy and Oscar were partners. Oscar was not a talker. Oscar was a thinker.

Then Miss Snodgrass went over the trip rules. There were A LOT of rules.

Miss Snodgrass was finally finished. It was time to get on the bus.

# Chapter Two
## Row, Row, Row Your Boat

Missy sat next to Oscar. Oscar sat next to the window.

Oscar told Missy all about the governor. . . .

Missy had heard enough about the governor. She wiggled in her seat. She looked around the bus.

Miss Snodgrass had said it would be a long bus ride. Missy didn't mind. There was lots to do.

Lily brought crackers—just in case she got carsick.

Dexter did magic tricks.

Taylor made something out of string.

Henry taught everyone a card game called crazy eights.

Nina and Nona showed off their matching socks.

And Samuel told about the time he ate seven hot dogs.

Yup, seven hot dogs!

When the bus screeched to a halt, the singing stopped. There was the state capitol. It was big—super duper BIG!

The students couldn't wait to get off the bus—especially Missy.

Before going inside, Miss Snodgrass reminded the students about the most important rule of the day.

# Chapter Three
## The Tour

Welcome to the capitol. My name is Miss Bertha.

Inside the capitol, the tour guide greeted Miss Snodgrass and her class.

Missy looked at Oscar. Then Oscar told Missy, "A rotunda is a round room."

The students saw lots of things on the tour . . .

a flag as big as a house,

a display of the state's birds,

a lot of old pots and arrowheads,

and a room full of old maps.

The students learned about the governor.

Missy began to wiggle and shuffle her feet. She had heard enough. She was ready for the gift shop.

Miss Bertha asked if anyone else wanted to guess. Missy smiled. She knew what the most important part of the tour was.

THE GIFT SHOP!

We always go to the gift shop before we get on the bus!

The gift shop?

No. There is no gift shop in the capitol.

35

After that, the tour just wasn't the same for Missy. But Miss Bertha kept talking.

All this talk about the governor and about laws gave Missy an idea.

We ARE going to meet the governor.

Yoo-hoo! Miss Snodgrass!

# Chapter Four
## Partners

Missy had a plan. Her plan did not include going to the bathroom.

You want to meet the governor, right?
Yes, but . . .
Oscar, remember the governor's motto? "Make it happen, and make it snappy!" Well, WE are going to make it happen! We are going to see the governor. And we don't have much time, so make it snappy!

Missy and Oscar looked for the governor's office. They found . . .

an old elevator,

a broom closet,

a man named Shorty,

and a conference room.

Missy sped down the hall. She was just about to open the door to the governor's office when Oscar stopped her.

Missy and Oscar walked up to the front desk.

A door opened, and a man looked out. It was the governor.

Missy and Oscar took a seat in the governor's office.

Now, what can I do for you two?

Missy got right to the point.

Well, Mr. Governor, sir, it's like this. You have a problem. A super duper BIG problem!

Mr. Governor, think about all the cool governor stuff you could have in a gift shop! Like . . . Um . . .

Just then, Oscar jumped up.

T-shirts that say "Make it happen, and make it snappy" and decoder rings and flashlights and state maps!

Missy looked the governor in the eye.

Well, Mr. Governor, what do you say?

The governor sat straight up in his chair.

His face lit up.

That's a TERRIFIC idea! A gift shop in the state capitol! I can see it now . . .

There will be key chains and bumper stickers! People will come by the busload!

LET'S PUT A GIFT SHOP IN THE CAPITOL!

When Missy and Oscar got up to leave, the governor gave Oscar a handshake and a campaign button that lit up.

The governor gave Missy a snow globe that played "The Star-Spangled Banner."

# Chapter Six
## Make It Snappy

As soon as the governor heard that Missy and Oscar needed to find their bus, he made things happen.

The governor led Missy and Oscar out of the capitol and down the steps. They marched across the street.

Once they got to the parking lot, it wasn't long before they found Miss Snodgrass and the rest of their class.

Everyone cheered!

And the bus driver honked the horn.

On the long bus ride home, Missy turned to Oscar.

Missy looked out the window.
One day she wanted to be a governor.
She would work in the capitol, and it
would have the best gift shop ever.
And her motto would be:

Make it happen,
make it snappy,
and make it—

# Super Duper
# Royal Deluxe!

The End